LOVE MOCKS A LIMP DICK

I0624616

By Donald W. Desaulniers

E-Book ISBN: 978-0-9920653-7-9
Paperback ISBN: 978-1-987888-45-4

Table of Contents

CHAPTER ONE (Little Lance)

I'm the world's worst fuck.

Pardon my salty language, but there's simply no better way to describe my affliction.

It's humiliating enough that my dick is absolutely unremarkable except for its vastly disappointing lack of length.

Even worse is the treachery of the little bastard. When I'm in bed jerking off, everything works like clockwork.

Put the little traitor within ten inches of real pussy, however, and it immediately droops like a deflated balloon, rendering it totally useless for its intended purpose.

Apparently some comedian came up with the line "I've outlived my penis" and that pretty much sums up what I've had to endure ever since I was a young man.

"Little Lance," as I've taken to calling him, obviously has the world's worst case of stage fright. Even an audience of one in a darkened bedroom is too much pressure for the disgusting little digit.

It's not all Little Lance's fault. I've never done anything to help him out.

I refuse to snort cocaine or smoke marijuana even though acquaintances have told me that both greatly enhance sex.

Doing drugs strikes me as nothing but fake fun and I'm about as honest a dude as you'll ever meet. There's nothing phony about me and I'm not about to get myself addicted to some drug just to get properly laid a few times, although sometimes I'm sorely tempted.

That same principle applies to my utter refusal to take Viagra or Cialis or any other of the legal penis stiffening drugs. Besides, I've always been leery of possible weird side effects. With my history of rotten luck, my nose might grow long and hard instead of Little Lance.

Ditto with seeing a shrink; Little Lance is my problem alone and the last thing I'd ever do is discuss my affliction with some stranger.

Trying to put a positive spin on the situation, Little Lance is my very effective line of defense against getting hooked up with the wrong woman. If he refuses to look inside the box, so to speak, then I can only assume that the woman isn't right for me.

I guess I consider Little Lance to be my top-of-the-line heartbreak repellant.

So far he's been perfect in that regard. I've never had my heart broken because I've never become close enough to a woman to fall in love.

Let me introduce myself.

I'm Lance Majestic, age fifty-nine, never engaged, never married, never been loved or been in love, although I've had countless crushes on pretty girls and women over the course of my lifetime. I just never had the nerve to tell the objects of my affection how I felt. I adored them from afar. It was much safer that way.

I live near downtown Las Vegas in a condominium apartment I purchased in 1995 when the real estate market was mired in a serious recession. It's fully paid for now and I never succumbed to the temptation of taking out my equity with some line of credit mortgage in order to temporarily improve my life style.

My job doesn't pay particularly well but then I'm not particularly qualified at my work either. I'm employed at an accountant's office in a small storefront right next door to my apartment building, but I'm not a certified accountant. I have an Honors Bachelor of Arts degree majoring in economics, but never bothered to pursue a CGA designation. I was appalled at the student loans I had already accumulated by the time I had finished my fourth and final year of university and decided to get myself a job right away rather than continue further with my education.

As a result I do all the work of an accountant except for signing the finished product. My boss has to sign all the financial statements prepared by me. He's happy because I earn about a third of what I would bring in if I had continued on in school and obtained a proper accountant's designation.

Only three of us work in the small office. Mike is the one and only accountant. I'm the sole assistant and Mike's wife, Myrtle, is the only secretary. Both of them are in their early seventies and I'll likely be out of a job once Mike retires or drops dead.

My apologies for beginning this story by disparaging my penis, but my latest humiliating failure is still fresh in my mind and I'm livid with Little Lance right now.

Before I tell you the gory details of last night's date, I've got to admit that I'm not a virgin.

In my fifty-nine years, I've actually been laid four times. Unfortunately I've failed to consummate twelve times.

Since I'm the one keeping score, then it's my call as to what constitutes a successful sexual encounter.

My four mild successes are as clear in my mind as if they happened yesterday. Even then, Little Lance proved to be more of a tease than a partner.

I sort of lost my virginity at age nineteen. The poor girl was only fifteen and I sincerely hope that I didn't ruin sex for her permanently.

We had been dating for a month or so while I was home from university for the summer. One night at a drive-in movie, we climbed into the back seat of the car and disrobed. I was as nervous as I'd ever been in my life.

Little Lance seemed to be functioning perfectly as I

attempted to guide him toward the ultimate goal line.

We weren't using any protection and as soon as Little Lance reached the threshold, he screamed at me to withdraw as he spewed out his prize all over the girl's naked thigh. It's highly unlikely that the encounter could accurately be described as penetration, but nevertheless I've always considered it to be my very first sexual conquest.

The girl and I dated twice more but wisely decided not to tempt fate again. Then it was time for me to return to university and I never saw her after that.

Embarrassingly, that was the most satisfying sexual episode of my whole sorry life and the only time I actually reached orgasm with a woman.

The remaining three scores were debasing one night stands fuelled by alcohol back in my early twenties, totally forgettable and unfulfilling for my partners but still precious treasures in my sex-starved mind.

My first eleven failures to launch are unfortunately also all permanently engrained in my memory. They all occurred back in my hometown of Kankakee, Illinois where I worked for the first nine years after graduating from college.

I have no idea why I couldn't perform properly, but the aftermath of those grisly encounters resulted in the insulting nicknames "Flopcock" and "Limp Dick" being paraded around town. Just when those embarrassing smears were finally fading from popularity, another dissatisfied date christened me with the horrible name "Sir Fuckslousy" and that humiliating moniker took off like a hit record. The snickers and general amusement that resulted from that starkly descriptive but unfortunately accurate disparagement caused me to quit my job and leave Kankakee in shame.

I worked in Utah for a year and then moved here to Las Vegas in 1986.

That's enough about my background. You've met both me and Little Lance. Now let me tell you about last night's fiasco.

CHAPTER TWO (Yet Another Failure)

After I left Kankakee, I virtually stopped dating.

I didn't see anyone at all in Utah and once I had settled here in Las Vegas, I kept pretty much to myself. I secured my current job within a month of moving to Nevada and it's always been just the three of us working here. One of the best places to find true love is at one's workplace, but that area of temptation doesn't apply to me. Myrtle, my only female co-worker, besides being fat and old, is already married to Mike.

Over the years I've had several women friends although we always tended to hang out in groups. I've avoided intimate dinners, using the line that I was a confirmed bachelor and prized my independence and solitude.

The difficulty with a single man maintaining a platonic friendship with a woman is the jealousy that crops up whenever that friend finds a romantic relationship. It's a rare man who is self-confident enough to permit his girl to continue seeing any friend who happens to be a guy. So far each of the female friendships I had nurtured ended permanently once a new man came into her life.

Lest I'm giving you the impression that I live a miserable life, let me assure you that I'm quite content with my situation. I genuinely enjoy my own company.

I long ago came to grips with the fact that each of us possesses various skills and that we also all have areas in which we're hopeless.

My area of ineptitude just happens to be in the bedroom.

Coincidentally, that's where I'm lying at this precise moment, wide awake even though it's three o'clock in the morning.

My date, Lori, left a couple of hours ago after making it crystal clear not to bother calling her again.

I'm once again totally mortified and my insomnia insists on making me relive this recent nightmare over and over again. I desperately want to fall asleep and put my failed erection out of my mind.

I've already warned Little Lance that if I'm not fast asleep by four o'clock, I'm going to get the scissors, sever the little traitor and flush him right down the toilet.

Overanalyzing last night's date, I really didn't do anything terribly wrong other than "limp out."

Lori and I met at a house party a couple of weeks ago on October 19th and immediately hit it off. She was perhaps a bit too young for me at age forty-two, but Lori was easy to talk to and seemed to enjoy my company.

I took her to a movie at Sam's Town the Saturday night after we met, and we played slots for a while afterwards.

Although my original intention was to seek a bit of social companionship rather than romance, Lori had obvious other plans and almost mauled me at her apartment door when I drove her home.

She more than implied that if her roommates hadn't been home, then Lori would have loved to have me come inside to continue our evening.

As I drove back home I was feeling almost giddy since I hadn't kissed a woman passionately in over twenty-five years.

Little Lance seemed fine with the idea as well and sprung up to his full three inches of power from the moment Lori's lips latched onto mine.

Lori and I had talked on the phone a couple of times this past week and I arranged to take her out for a nice dinner on Saturday evening, being last night.

Perhaps it was unwise to order a full liter of wine, but that was Lori's idea.

The meal at the top of Binion's was fantastic and I was quite enjoying myself.

By the time we ordered a second bottle of wine, I was mildly apprehensive. Lori had thrown back far more wine than I had, and her conversation was beginning to demonstrate that she was a bit rough around the edges. Both her language and grammar had drifted down more than a few notches and it was apparent that her previous demure and refined personality had been a bit of a performance.

Still, Lori was blond, slim and quite pretty, and I found myself very much physically attracted to her.

She clung to me as we walked the three blocks to my apartment.

"What a lovely place you have, Lance!" she exclaimed as we entered my unit.

"Thanks, Lori. I really like it here. As I mentioned earlier, I work right next door so I never have to worry about traffic or weather. Not too many guys can brag that their daily commute is less than a hundred feet."

I showed Lori around the spacious condo including my bedroom and the second, slightly smaller bedroom which I used as a home office.

My three cats, Wilnot, Fluffy, and Little Grey were considerate enough to stay in the spare room and not bother us. Although it may have been just my imagination, I thought Lori threw me an odd look when she spotted the three sleeping cats.

"Would you like a coffee or something?" I inquired.

"A liqueur would be great," Lori answered.

I showed her what I had in stock and she selected Kahlua straight up. I poured us each a drink but added a bit of milk to my own.

Lori excused herself to use the bathroom and I put on a Leonard

Cohen CD with another by Bob Dylan
to follow automatically.

When she returned to the living-
room, Lori looked quite stunning.
She had fixed her make-up and
taken off her sweater, revealing a
very low-cut and sexy blouse.

After a couple of sips of our
drinks, Lori leaned over and
kissed me softly on the lips. I
was quite thrilled with this turn
of events.

Then, dispensing with any more
preliminaries, Lori stood up and
held out both hands. I stretched
both arms out in front of me and
Lori grabbed my hands and pulled
me upwards.

She smiled hungrily as she led
me slowly toward my darkened
bedroom.

As Lori pushed the door open,
the already soft light from the
living-room illuminated the
bedroom slightly.

She continued to guide me toward
the bed. When we reached the
bedside, Lori began to remove my
clothing ever so slowly.

It was all quite wonderful and sensations I hadn't felt in decades began overpowering me.

Once she had undressed me down to my underpants, Lori performed her own intimate and scintillating striptease and continued until she was stark naked and absolutely ravishing in the semi-darkness.

That turned out to be the apex of the evening, the optimum point of my arousal and enjoyment.

Everything after that sweetest of moments went rapidly downhill.

Lori knelt down and slowly eased my undershorts down my legs. I dutifully lifted one leg and then the other to allow her to remove this last vestige of my clothing.

That tantalizing chore completed, Lori, still on her knees, lifted her gaze and blurted out the most hurtful words a guy could ever hear.

"My God, you're so tiny. My last boyfriend was from Jamaica. I've never seen such a puny penis."

I didn't know how to respond so I joked, "Well, Lori, if the average guy has six inches, then for every three inch midget like me, some lucky guy gets blessed with a nine inch weapon."

Perhaps it was the booze, or maybe just the shock of seeing Little Lance up close and personal, but Lori didn't laugh at my self-deprecating wit.

Luckily for me, she didn't run out of the room either. I was still hopeful that I'd get the gold and for a moment it appeared that victory might still be imminent.

Lori guided me onto the bed and lay down beside me.

"Even though this is only our second date, Lance, you won't find me too hard to seduce. I want to feel you inside me."

That was the exact moment when Little Lance decided to go on strike. As a result, Lori didn't find me too hard either.

She gave it her best shot for a few minutes, unsuccessfully attempting to stuff the world's shortest and limpest penis into her wet and waiting love-nest, but it was futile.

Finally in her intoxicated exasperation, Lori snarled, "What's the matter with you? Are you queer or something?"

"I'm so sorry, Lori. I must be nervous. It's a travesty because you're so sexy and gorgeous right now. I told you I hadn't dated for a long time."

"What a waste!" Lori spat out as she quickly got up from the bed and scooped up her clothes. "I'm horny. How the fuck am I supposed to find a real man at this hour of the night? Thanks for nothing, Lance. Don't bother contacting me ever again. You're as useless as that sorry excuse you call a dick."

"I really am sorry, Lori. Let me call you a cab?"

I had never seen anyone dress so quickly.

"Fuck off. I'll find my own. I can't stand even looking at your pathetic mug for another second."

With that final insult, Lori was out the door.

I locked it and forlornly slunk back into my bedroom.

That was two hours ago and here I still am in my bed, totally humiliated and dejected.

Never again will I try to have sex.

CHAPTER THREE (Anger Management)

Luckily I fell asleep before four o'clock. I was morose enough to actually slice Little Lance to shreds to show him I hadn't been kidding when I issued my threat to him.

All three cats must have sensed my despair, because they eventually jumped up onto my bed and consoled me. Knowing that at least they loved me permitted me finally to drift off into dreamland.

The next day was Sunday so I didn't have to drag my dejected carcass into work.

It was impossible to put the failed episode out of my mind. I tried to divert my attention by thoroughly cleaning the apartment but that only killed a couple of hours after breakfast.

Although I rarely gamble, around one o'clock I walked over to the Golden Nugget and played keno

slots until suppertime and only
lost about thirty bucks while
slowly drinking several
complimentary bottles of beer.

I grabbed supper at the
McDonald's in the D Las Vegas
hotel and got back home just after
seven.

TV actually wasn't bad and I
found an action movie to keep me
occupied, along with more beer,
until I hit the sack just after
eleven.

I was actually looking forward
to getting back to work in the
morning. I had a complicated set
of financial statements to prepare
in order to complete a file for
Mike's Tuesday morning appointment
with his client.

My bedside telephone rattled me
awake at one o'clock in the
morning. The cats scrambled off
the bed.

"Hello," I mumbled into the
receiver, still feeling somewhat
intoxicated from all the beer.

A drunken female voice snarled
back at me.

"Wake up, Spaghetti Dick. It's time to check your cock for a pulse."

It wasn't Lori's voice but obviously she was there. I heard snickers and giggles in the background.

"Aren't you the funny little comedian, Lori? Go back to your party and stop bothering me."

I hung up.

Thirty minutes later the damn phone rang again.

"What now?" I sighed.

A chorus of voices chanted "TINY, TINY, TINY" amid a cacophony of inebriated laughter.

A woman's voice then taunted, "You're on speaker phone, Tiny. What words of wisdom can the world's smallest pecker bestow upon us?"

I felt anger billowing up inside me. By now I had a hangover headache but I tried to control my temper.

"Are you idiots fifteen years old? Stop harassing me in the middle of the night."

I slammed the receiver back down.

This time I couldn't get back to sleep. Memories of my tormentors back in Kankakee flooded back. Obviously I had forgotten the cruel lessons learned back then. It was a mistake to have taken Little Lance out on a sex-walk again. I should have kept him in permanent storage. It was quickly becoming apparent that I had disappointed the wrong woman. Lori was already sharing my shortcomings with all her friends.

The phone blared again.

I reluctantly answered it.

A giggly female voice announced, "Hello, my name is Anita Dick. You're on speaker phone. My friends and I are looking for a cheap three-inch thrill. Have we come to the right place?"

I went on the offensive.

"Yes you have, Anita. But first, let me tell you about your friend, Lori Irwin. Spending time with her was definitely thrilling. In the course of one evening and two bottles of wine, I witnessed her complete deterioration from a refined, seemingly intelligent lady into a cheap, sex-addicted trollop. It was most fortunate for me that my little penis saw right through her charade and refused to go inside for a closer inspection. Lord knows what vile diseases the little guy and I would have contracted. I hope you're not sharing a glass or a needle with that low-class slut. I'm sure that Lori is infested with either crabs or bedbugs. I've had to wash my sheets four times since she barged out of here in her drunken stupor. It's been lovely chatting with you Anita. Tell Lori what a pleasure it's been to have met her and her pet crabs."

I hung up before anyone could respond and then I turned the ringer off to prevent any more disruptions.

One piece of wisdom actually did expose itself. I realized that being taunted about one's lack of sexual prowess didn't hurt nearly as much at age fifty-nine as it did when I was a young man.

I had mixed feelings about my outburst. One part of me felt that some sort of snappy comeback had definitely been justified, but another part was a bit apprehensive about what Pandora's Box I might have inadvertently opened.

I sincerely hoped that Lori didn't turn out to be a nut job.

CHAPTER FOUR (Sandwich Board Revenge)

My headache was still in evidence when I woke up at eight o'clock on Monday morning. I made some toast and coffee and hauled myself off to work.

I had the office to myself all day. Mike and Myrtle had gone to Los Angeles for the weekend to visit their daughter and had left me in charge of the office.

It took me until well after five o'clock to complete the paperwork for Mike's Tuesday morning appointment.

I had skipped lunch so treated myself to supper at the buffet in the Golden Nugget.

To ensure that my sleep wouldn't be interrupted again, I turned the telephone ringer off when I got into bed. I'm remarkably old fashioned and refuse to bring myself fully into the realm of modern technology. I've never owned or wanted a cell phone and my TV was the older style, but since it still worked fine, I saw no need to purchase a trendy flat screen in order to get a high definition picture.

My telephone service was very basic and I have always shunned call display or any type of answering machine. Most of my calls were unwanted cold calls anyway and I saw no need to preserve them until I got back home. My few friends knew enough to keep calling back until I was home. If it was important, they could always reach me at the office.

I sat in with Mike on Tuesday morning and helped explain to the client the details of the annual financial statements for his businesses. That took all morning and then some.

Mike and I walked to the Plaza and had a late lunch there.

As we returned to the office and were about a block and a half away, Mike noticed someone with one of those old-fashioned sandwich board advertising contraptions hung around his neck near our office.

"Wonder what that's all about?" he asked. "It's a strange place to advertise. There's hardly any sidewalk traffic."

"He must be touting a nearby pizza parlor or something," I responded. "The cars going by can easily see what he's peddling."

We saw some cars slow down as they approached the sign and a couple of them tooted their horns.

Mike and I looked at each other quizzically.

"Whatever he's selling, the sign is certainly attracting attention," Mike commented.

By now we were about fifty feet away.

"He's right in front of our office," Mike said. "I hope he's not protesting anything I've done."

"I can't imagine that we've irritated any client, Mike. All our work is pretty mundane."

Mike's eyes were sharper than mine.

Suddenly he blurted out "What the Hell?" and began to laugh.

By now all the cars passing on either side of the street were slowing to a crawl in order to see what the fuss was about.

I gasped when the words on the sign finally became readable.

The deadbeat wearing it stopped before turning around to face us.

That back side of the sign blared out in large lettering the words, "HOME OF THE WORLD'S WORST FUCK."

I knew immediately that Lori was getting her revenge and I rued my saucy words spewed out on the phone the other night to the woman calling herself Anita Dick.

The old guy slowly turned around. Mike and I were now stopped dead in our tracks ten feet away, both dumbfounded by the scathing castigation on the billboard.

"I sure hope that's not Myrtle's handiwork," Mike joked.

The front side of the sign suddenly appeared, and it was even more personal.

"LANCE MAJESTIK HAS A TINY USELESS DICK" was the public message on that end of the board.

Mike broke out laughing. When he had finally composed himself, he bantered, "Can't wait to hear this story, Lance. Let's go inside and you can tell Myrtle and me what you've done to warrant such a vicious attack."

I decided right then and there not to let the situation upset me, no matter what indignity might yet be on the horizon.

"At least she's spared no expense," I joked. "It's a very professional sign. The lettering is immaculate."

I addressed the old gent sporting the sandwich board.

"Hello, sir. I'm Lance, the target of your employer's wrath. May I ask how long you're being paid to lug it around?"

The fellow appeared embarrassed but from the look of him, any job was better than no job at all.

"I'll get fifty bucks if I walk up and down in front of this office until five o'clock as long as I return the sign in good condition."

"When did you get here?" Mike asked.

"Just after one o'clock."

"If you get thirsty, tap on the window and we'll bring you a soft drink," I replied.

Mike and I went inside the office. Myrtle was both appalled and exceedingly curious at the same time, something akin to people rubbernecking their way past a gruesome accident scene.

I explained what had happened on Saturday night and also about the crank calls late on Sunday night.

I could tell that Myrtle felt terrible for me but had no inkling how best to respond. Mike didn't show the least bit of sympathy. He thought the whole situation was hilarious.

I tried to reassure Myrtle.

"Don't worry about it, Myrtle. When I was much younger back home in Illinois, getting teased about my lack of endowment was soul shattering and caused me to leave town in shame. I'm a grown man now and I'm determined not to let this circus get to me. I'm fine. At this precise moment I'm not sure what if anything I'm going to do about that awful sign, but apparently the old fellow will only be lugging it around until five o'clock. Now please excuse me. I'm going into my office to slit my wrists."

Since I was smiling when I said it, Mike knew it was a joke and broke out in howls of laughter. Myrtle just stood there in a state of shock.

I closed my door behind me and pondered what to do.

Suddenly I was struck with a brilliant idea. The best defense was a good offense.

I exited my office and went into the supply room. For the next thirty minutes I worked feverishly while inspiration flooded my imagination.

Finally my masterpiece was ready. I had created my own sandwich board using white cardboard, sturdy string and heavy black marker.

I refused to show my handiwork to Mike or Myrtle when I emerged from the supply room.

Instead I went back outside and fitted my concoction over my head so that it hung properly.

On the back side I had emblazoned in gargantuan lettering the words, "HI, I'M LANCE MAJESTIK."

On the front side I belted out the slogan, "THREE INCHES OF PURE FUN. CALL ME ANYTIME."

Undaunted by the attention my own billboard would undoubtedly attract, I began marching up and down in front of the office.

Mike and Myrtle came out to see what I was up to. Myrtle was appalled and tried to persuade me to come back inside. Mike, on the other hand, was like a kid at a carnival and began snapping pictures of the two competing sandwich boards on his cellphone.

Within half an hour a news van stopped just up the street and a crew jumped out and approached us.

By now a small crowd was beginning to accumulate.

The news team also began taking pictures of the dueling billboards.

Once they were satisfied that they had captured the visual uniqueness of the demonstration, the pretty news lady began interviewing the old drunk while the cameras rolled.

I couldn't hear what the old guy was saying because I continued to march up and down the sidewalk.

Cars were now actually stopping to take their own pictures of the bizarre scene, causing a veritable traffic jam.

When the news crew was finished with my counterpart, they turned their attention to me.

With the camera and microphone pointed directly at me, I stopped to allow the team to conduct the interview.

"Sir, can you explain what occurred to cause someone to go to the trouble of launching such a purposeful protest against you?"

"I believe, ma'am, that the lady's billboard explains her complaint fully and graphically."

Both the cameraman and interviewer were having a difficult time restraining their smiles and giggles. The news lady was pursing her lips in a vain attempt to look serious.

"What made you decide to make up your own rebuttal sandwich board?" the woman finally squeaked out breathlessly.

"I chose to use the situation to drum up some more great dates. In the bedroom, I'm not happy until my date's not happy."

"Are you considering legal action against the disgruntled lady who made that insulting billboard?"

"I'd lose the lawsuit. She'd successfully defend my action by claiming that each statement was absolutely true."

"Let me get this straight. Are you really admitting that you're terrible in the sack?"

"I'm obviously worse than terrible. Have you ever heard of any other badly seduced woman going to such lengths to proclaim just how awful her experience actually was? In the bedroom disappointment department, I'm number one. I believe my latest date's graphic response speaks for itself."

That ended the interview. The news lady asked me for Lori's name and address, which I provided on the express condition that they not be used unless Lori consented.

I wasn't the least bit embarrassed by this turn of events. Las Vegas was a huge city and very few people knew me here.

I even derived a bit of satisfaction wondering how Lori would react to this totally unexpected development. Don't mess with Lance Majestik unless you're willing to flush all your own dignity down the toilet. He certainly doesn't care about his.

After the news team left and the crowd dispersed, I went back into the office.

The old drunk continued to prance up and down until five o'clock. Once he had left his post, I decided to go home.

Mike and Myrtle were still working when I told them I was calling it a day.

"I sure hope you know what you're doing," Mike admonished as I opened the door to leave.

"I haven't got a clue, Mike. Everything was ad-lib. I just decided that I wasn't going to let that crazy bitch humiliate me any longer. Enough is enough."

CHAPTER FIVE (Mr. Infamous)

My belligerence quickly subsided once I got inside my own apartment and I felt quite shell-shocked. Lori's insulting display had goaded me into revealing my deepest and darkest secret to the whole world.

I cooked my own supper and put the local news on at six o'clock.

The lead story was a classic. Close up and personal, but with the letters "UC" in the word "FUCK" tastefully obscured, the old fellow was shown marching up and down the sidewalk.

He was interviewed explaining that a pretty blond lady had given him the sign and promised to pay him fifty dollars if he carried it past the accountant's office until five o'clock and then returned the sign.

My own interview in full was then aired, although it took less than a minute.

The same news lady who had attended at the scene concluded the piece by stating that the woman responsible for the sign had been contacted but declined to contribute any more to the story.

With the screen vividly displaying me and my sign while she spoke, the announcer then signed off by warning, "Men, be careful who you sleep with. Your performance may be graded and found to be lacking. Don't end up like this poor guy."

When the news station switched cameras back to the anchor, he couldn't restrain his amusement and lost his composure completely by breaking into uncontrollable laughter. The station had to run to commercial immediately.

My own telephone continued to ring all evening. Most of the calls were from people I knew. I made light of the whole event even in those instances in which my friends appeared to feel sorry for me.

There was no point backing down now.

It was most unfortunate that I was the only "Majestik" listed in the Las Vegas phone directory.

Several of the calls were of the crank variety and obviously emanated from bored or mischievous teenagers. Even with those conversations I maintained my sense of humor and laughed right along with the callers. I urged each of them to learn from my misfortune.

At eleven o'clock when I went to bed, I wisely turned off the ringer.

The next day was surreal.

A video of the newscast had "gone viral" as the young people say, and had generated over a million "hits" by noon. The sidewalk in front of our office was inundated with onlookers, and more media types soon came lurking around.

"I'm really sorry for the upheaval, Mike. Do you want me to take the rest of the day off?"

"No way! This is the most excitement Myrtle and I have ever had. Look at all the free publicity I'm getting. We'll soon be as famous as those pawn shop stars."

"Except we'll be known as the porn stars," Myrtle chimed in.

It wasn't easy getting any real work done, but then November is a reasonably quiet time in an accountant's world so nothing we had on tap was absolutely urgent.

A well-dressed gentleman entered the offices just after three o'clock and asked to speak with me. Myrtle ushered him into my office and closed the door behind her.

"Yes, sir; how can I help you?"

"I'm Brian Kirkwood with the Fat Freddy Friday Comedy Hour production. I'm sure you've heard of our show."

"Yes, sir; I often watch it on Friday night."

"We'd like to have you on this Friday's show. It gets taped here in our Las Vegas studio tomorrow morning."

"I don't know, Brian. I'm not really a funny guy. I'm sure I'd bomb out as a comedian."

"Don't worry. Freddy is world class at moving interviews along and making them humorous. He'll do all the work. Everything gets thoroughly edited as well, so by the time the final tape is ready, you'll seem like a natural born funny man. Your rather unique display yesterday was hilarious and it's still fresh in everybody's mind. Trust me. It will make for a great segment on the show."

Despite some serious misgivings about allowing the fiasco with Lori to escalate even further, I reluctantly agreed to give it a try. I must have been out of my mind because I certainly wasn't any type of publicity hound.

Mike was thrilled when I informed him I was taking the next day off in order to be taped for Fat Freddy's show.

I really did enjoy that weekly
show. It was quite ribald but,
combined with a few beer on a
lonely Friday night, watching
Freddy and his outrageous antics
made the time melt away.

For supper I had a sixteen inch
meat lover's pizza and two huge
drafts of Old Town Brown dark ale
at Magnolia's in the Four Queens.

No one recognized me at my tiny
table for one in the back section
of the restaurant.

On Wednesday morning I drove to
the recording studio where an
assistant applied the necessary
stage make-up in an attempt to
make me look natural for the
camera. For my age, I'm not bad
looking. My full head of hair is
still sandy with just a touch of
grey at the temples and I'm six
feet tall and quite slender. I'm
certainly not handsome but I'm not
hideous-looking either.

Fat Freddy came in just before
ten o'clock, introduced himself
and insisted on getting started
immediately.

I was seated on a sofa beside Freddy's desk and he assured me that these types of interviews worked out best if there were no pre-arranged questions or answers.

"Complete spontaneity produces the best results," he added. "Don't be nervous and try to ignore the cameras. It's just two guys having a casual conversation."

He waved to the cameramen to begin rolling and Freddy looked directly at me.

"The word on the street, Lance, is that you're a terrible fuck. Do you mind explaining why women are saying that?"

I decided to play right along.

"It's a gift, Freddy. Some guys can write a fantastic novel in a week but they can't even pound a nail into a board without screwing up. I can prepare your income tax return perfectly no matter how messed up your records are, but I can't satisfy a woman in the sack no matter how drunk I might get her."

Freddy was obviously most pleased with my answer and I could see his huge face light up with anticipation.

"Just how bad can you be in bed, Lance?"

"That's hard to quantify, Freddy. None of my victims has ever returned for an encore. I can honestly state that no woman has ever complimented me on my bedroom performance."

"Could it possibly be your equipment, Lance? You seem to have come up a bit short according to that young lady's billboard."

"That's a valid point, Freddy. I clearly explained the law of averages to my date the other night when she said I had the tiniest penis she'd ever seen."

"Tell the viewers what you mean."

"Look," I answered, "it comes down to this. If the average guy has six inches, then for every three inch twiddler like mine, somebody out there must have a nine inch magnifico."

Freddy himself burst out laughing. Then he responded. "Women say that length doesn't matter. Even guys with tiny dicks claim to get laid all the time."

"Freddy, you can't get to the top of the list of lousy screws with just a single deficiency."

"I see. What other shortcomings do you have that got your date so riled up that she hired a professional sign maker and then paid an old gent to parade around airing her beefs for the world to see?"

"You've got to have an effective one-two punch, Freddy. Besides sporting a tiny instrument, a guy needs something else to thoroughly disappoint a woman in the sack."

"And what's your secret weapon?"

"My penis likes to be called 'Little Lance' but he has the worst possible case of stage fright. He's like a soldier all raring for combat when he heads off to war but who falls down and surrenders when he gets his first whiff of real action."

"Have you always had this problem?"

"For ever and ever, and believe me, it has led to some awful nicknames."

"Care to share a few?"

"Sorry, but it's still too painful to talk about. Your viewers can probably guess some of those names which permanently hurt Little Lance's feelings. I was born with next to nothing and I've come to grips with that sad fact. Not all guys can be hung like a bull chipmunk. Getting called noxious names was devastating when I was younger."

"Come on, our time is almost up. Tell us the most hurtful nickname you've ever had hung on you and then I'll let you go."

I paused for a moment and then answered, "That would definitely be Sir Fuckslousy."

Fat Freddy ended the segment by apologizing to his female viewers that censorship laws prevented him from having me introduce Little Lance to the world.

"Thank God for that," I shouted. "Goodnight, Freddy."

Both Freddy and his producer thanked me profusely for doing the interview and assured me that the finished product which would air on Friday night would be great.

CHAPTER SIX (My Fifteen Minutes of Fame)

I refused to tell Mike and Myrtle what had taken place in Freddy's studio.

"You guys will just have to tune in to the show this Friday," I insisted.

"We'll not only watch it," Mike responded, "but we'll be taping it as well. I'd suggest you do the same thing. It's a real honor to get on Freddy's show. You're going to be famous."

"I think the more accurate word is 'infamous' but hardly anyone knows me around here anyway. Doing the show is my way of ensuring that from now on women will just leave me alone. My experience on Saturday night wasn't just horrible for my date. I'm sure it was far more traumatic for me."

The phone calls were scarce on Wednesday night and again I turned the ringer off when I hit the sack.

Thursday was uneventful at the office. Very few gawkers walked by and no media types.

I was extremely grateful that I didn't work in a big office. I could only imagine the "short" jokes and assorted snide comments that would quickly be passed around the water cooler.

No one phoned on Thursday evening so I didn't bother to turn the ringer off when I got into bed at half past eleven.

That turned out to be unwise.

The telephone blared to life and roused me out of a deep sleep at quarter past one.

It was Lori and her gang of drunks again.

A female began the crank call by saying in a slurred voice, "Now you've gone and made a total moron of yourself, you limp-dicked loser."

Although she was attempting to disguise her voice, I recognized that it was Lori herself.

"You started it, Lori, paying that old drunk to strut around with the demeaning billboard hanging around his neck. I bet you never thought I'd manage to turn the tables and make you look like a mean, bitchy idiot."

"Shut up. You're on speaker phone. It's you who looks like the pathetic loser you really are. I simply stood up for all the disappointed and defrauded women of America when I made your joke of a pecker a public laughing stock."

The ladies obviously appreciated that comeback and cheered.

"Well, Lori, if you and your army of lesbian alkies can tear yourselves away from your circle jerk on Friday night, we'll see who gets the last laugh. Make sure you tune in to Fat Freddy's Comedy Hour."

With that adolescent retort, I hung up the phone and turned off the ringer.

I was moderately pleased with myself. No woman can out-gross a guy.

Mike and I had lunch at the Plaza on Friday and two middle-aged men came up to us, mentioned that they had seen the newscast about the billboards, and commiserated about how mean some women could be. They congratulated me on fighting back. I told them to watch Fat Freddy's show tonight.

I programmed my TV to tape the show while I watched it at the same time, and I was tremendously proud of my performance, although the four cans of beer I drank might have contributed to my rave self-review.

Freddy had edited the show masterfully and interspersed some hilariously distasteful jokes about women at different intervals during my interview.

Occasionally in prior shows Freddy had made cracks about the ladies in order to titillate his mostly male viewers, but tonight he really pushed the envelope.

I came across as a nice guy who had been savaged by a vicious bitch, and because of that portrayal, the call-in comments and on-line tweets were more than 90 percent supportive of me and critical of Lori's behavior.

During the last portion of the show, Freddy had a totally outrageous local comedian doing a ten minute monologue about what harpies most women can be. Some of his comments were both obscene and hilarious at the same time. I literally couldn't stop laughing. Although I'm certain the fellow mostly used an existing routine, he had purposely up-dated it with some great lines referring specifically to me and Lori.

As a special dig at Lori and aggressively critical women like her, the comedian had a skit in which an old guy paraded around with a sandwich board in front of a hairdressing salon. On the front was the slogan "HOME OF THE

WORLD'S WORST BLOW JOB." The back sported the sarcastic phrase "GINNY SMITH HAS THE WORLD'S GROSSEST BOX." The old man was cleverly shown marching back and forth in the background during the whole segment while Naughty Al, the comedian, told raunchy jokes about huge, well-worn vaginas and the debilitating penis and tongue injuries that guys encounter when they come into close contact with the dreaded "dry hole." To make it even funnier, women inside the hair salon were shown throwing the finger at the sandwich board guy and making other threatening gestures at him.

The show ended at one o'clock in the morning and within two minutes my telephone rang.

It was a livid, drunk and obscene Lori threatening to sue my ass off. In the background I could hear other ladies calling me filthy names.

I probably should have tried to calm the waters but by then I had polished off at least six beer, so instead of being contrite, I repeated one of Naughty Al's most outrageous lines from the skit.

That absolutely enraged the roomful of already pissed off women. I realized that Lori had put me on speaker phone so I stirred the pot further by announcing, "I hereby call to order this meeting of the Lesbian Army. Okay fellow bitches, now everyone raise her dildo high in the air and repeat after me. Men are superior beings. We must always accommodate their most perverted requests. Men rule this planet and it is hopeless to think we can defeat them."

I then began laughing mockingly.

"Don't for a minute think that this war is over, Sir Fuckslousy. We're only getting started."

With that pronouncement, Lori hung up on me.

In my thoroughly inebriated state, I foolishly believed that I had already won the war. I turned the phone ringer off and collapsed into bed.

Saturday and Sunday were the strangest days I had ever lived through.

My phone literally rang off the hook from morning until I shut off the ringer at night.

Most of the calls were from guys congratulating me on getting such full and complete revenge against the woman who had gone out of her way to humiliate me publicly.

About a quarter of the calls were from angry women who tore a strip off me for allowing the situation to be used by Fat Freddy as a vehicle to denigrate women. I tried to be polite as I assured each lady that Freddy's single show was to be my one and only claim to my fifteen minutes of fame, and that I had decided not to partake in any additional media interviews or other public displays.

The remaining few calls were from various media outlets wanting me to grant them interviews or appear on their shows. I respectfully declined their requests. A couple of those callers were even willing to pay for my appearance but I still said no. The situation had already gotten way out of hand.

CHAPTER SEVEN (The War Intensifies)

I was merely an accountant's assistant and had no previous experience with media or controversy.

Monday at the office was next to impossible because of repeated phone calls, all wanting to speak with me about Freddy's show. We didn't receive even one business related call all morning. Two news vans and loads of people were lurking around in front of the building.

Mike called me into his office just before lunch.

"You've really opened up a can of worms, Lance. Our customers can't even contact us because our telephone is constantly busy. I've received four E-mails already cancelling appointments. The last thing most of my clients want is to be forced to fight their way through a media circus in order to get their taxes done."

"I'm really sorry about it, Mike. How could I know that one simple act of impulsiveness on my part could have such enormous unintended consequences? Believe me, I never would have charged outside with my own billboard if I had known that this chaos would ensue. Would you like me to take the week off? I haven't used all of my vacation yet."

"I think that would be wise. If the situation is still abominable by next Monday then we'll have to talk. If my business is going to plunge down the toilet because of this thing, then Myrtle and I might just as well close it up. She's been after me for the past few years to retire while we've still got our health."

I left the office and fought my way through the small crowd. I had intended to go straight to my apartment but when the people began following me, I decided to go downtown and grab some lunch, so I quickly crossed Main Street and doubled back toward the Plaza.

Like a swarm of fish, the crowd pursued me. Some of them were much faster and by the time I reached the bus station, my way was blocked.

That delay enabled the two news cameramen to catch up. With both cameras rolling, the first reporter arrived and breathlessly asked if I had received any reaction regarding Fat Freddy's show on Friday night.

Being so inexperienced in the spotlight, and given my naturally polite personality, I didn't realize that I could have kept my mouth shut and just pushed my way through the people.

"Yes, ma'am. I've received countless phone calls, both at my apartment on the weekend and back there at my office this morning. I'm taking the rest of the week off in the hopes that the whole sorry matter will be forgotten. We can't get any work done with the constant disruptions."

"Are the calls supportive or critical of you?"

"The women callers invariably made negative comments but every single male who phoned was enthusiastically supportive of what I did to try to turn the tables on the disgruntled lady who attacked me through that demeaning sandwich board."

Before the reporter could ask another question, someone in the crowd yelled out, "Hey newspaper lady, bring your camera over here and get a load of this."

Curious myself, I followed the crew over to the far end of the bus station building.

The people, most of whom were laughing, parted to enable the news crew to gain close access.

I gasped when it dawned on me what I was looking at.

A poster had been taped to the bus station's window.

It showed my head shot superimposed over a nude male body whose almost non-existent penis was clearly displayed.

Underneath in large print were the words, "LANCE MAJESTIK. BIG SEDUCTION TALK. PATHETIC PENIS. DON'T FALL FOR HIS LIES. HE COMES UP VERY SHORT."

While the crew got several close-up shots of the poster, someone nearby called out, "Here's another one and it's different."

The crew along with the swarm of onlookers darted over to the second poster. The disgusting picture was identical but this one bore the slogan, "LANCE MAJESTIK. BIG PROMISES. NO PENIS."

The news lady had the cameraman point the lens back at me as she asked, "Mr. Majestik, what is your reaction to these posters?"

Humiliation definitely clouds one's mind. Despite my earlier resolve not to comment further, this latest attack floored me, so I launched my own offensive.

"Look, no one could feel worse than I did when Little Lance went on strike and refused to perform in the sack. I'm truly sorry that my date was so disappointed with my failure to satisfy her. But these posters are obscene. It's my head shot but someone else's body. The disgruntled lady and some of her female friends have been calling me in the middle of the night in order to wake me up and call me debasing names, both before and after Fat Freddy's show last Friday night. I call them the Lesbian Army. If this type of gross criticism is what guys can expect whenever they don't meet a woman's expectations in the bedroom, then most of us may as well give up all hope of ever finding a quality woman to love us, especially those of us who are not well endowed."

"What do you intend to do about these posters?" the reporter queried.

"I'm going to tear them down whenever I find them, but other than that, I'd be crazy to escalate this war in any way. I admit defeat. There's no way a mild-mannered guy like me can defeat an army of sexually frustrated witches who'll stop at nothing to humiliate their male enemy."

This particular poster was taped to the outside of a window so I peeled it off while the cameras were still rolling and ripped it into pieces with an exaggerated flourish. The predominantly male crowd cheered.

I then proceeded into the Plaza and lost the remnants of the crowd in the busy casino.

My next stop was at a costume shop on Fremont Street East where I purchased a wig and beard ensemble.

Lori and her friends didn't even wait until after midnight to taunt me.

She called just before ten o'clock and slurred, "What's up, Poster Boy? Or rather, what's not up, Father Flaccid?"

Her female audience roared approval in the background.

"You and your cronies have gone way too far, Lori. Those posters are disgusting. I hope you get charged for public indecency. Do you pathetic women get plastered every night? No wonder none of you can ever keep a man. You're nothing but a gang of drunken sluts."

I knew as soon as I spat out that insult that it was a mistake, but it was too late to retract it.

"The best is yet to come, Sir Fuckslousy," Lori retorted angrily before slamming the receiver down in my ear.

Monday must have been an extremely slow news day, because Tuesday morning's local newspaper blared out at the top of the front page, "LESBIAN ARMY ATTACKS."

The two posters and their insulting slogans were prominently displayed under the headline, and my full name was used throughout the article. "My" genital area was blacked out like Elvis Presley's hips on the Ed Sullivan Show back in the fifties.

My quotation about the Lesbian Army led off the article, which then recapped the entire "War of the Sexes" as the reporter had deemed to dub it.

Fat Freddy's show was summarized as was Lori's billboard attack and my response.

I'm sure that if this had occurred back in Kankakee when I was thirty years of age, I would have committed suicide.

It was fortunate that by age fifty-nine, I had come to grips with my sexual inabilities. In my mind I now represented impotent men of all ages.

The bizarre fight was beginning to receive wider attention because both Leno and Letterman made extensive jokes about it in their monologues on Tuesday night.

Leno opined that any guy with the name Lance Majestik was bound to disappoint the ladies when they discovered that he sported a three inch penis.

Letterman even used the story for his "Top Ten List," which he called "Ten things a guy doesn't want to hear after he fails to perform."

They were all quite hilarious, and the final or worst thing was "The Lesbian Army is here to see you."

CHAPTER EIGHT (Out of a Job)

Mike phoned on Wednesday morning and asked if he could come up to my apartment.

When he arrived, his expression was very glum. I knew the news wouldn't be good.

"Myrtle and I can't handle this awful situation, Lance. We've decided to close up the office permanently. The Grainger Group over on Ogden Street has agreed to take over any of my clients who are willing to switch to them and they've already cut the check to purchase my business. They don't have an opening for you because they don't want that kind of publicity. You've been with me a long time, Lance, and I feel terrible about abandoning you while you're right in the middle of this mess. I've prepared a check to cover your wages, unused vacation pay and two month's salary in lieu of notice. I sincerely wish you all the best and hope that you'll accept this check in full satisfaction of what we owe you. Myrtle and I can't afford to fight you in court about adequate severance and the whole situation is too bizarre. My lawyer can't even answer the legal question about whether what you've done constitutes something for which we can justifiably sack you for cause with no severance."

"I'm so sorry about the whole mess, Mike. Of course I'll accept your check and not pursue any claim against you. You're my friend and I've enjoyed working with you all these years. Please don't let this episode tarnish our friendship. When do the Grainger people take over your practice?"

"They're coming to get our files and all the office equipment later this afternoon. Myrtle and I have been frantically calling all our clients to let them know that we're retiring immediately. Can you come back with me now and get all your personal effects? The landlord has someone who wants to take over our offices on Friday, which means we don't have to worry about breaking our lease."

I walked back to Mike's offices and packed my personal stuff in two boxes. Myrtle hugged me and promised to keep in touch.

"In some ways you've done us a huge favor, Lance. The chaos resulting from the billboard incident finally enabled me to convince Mike to call it quits. We're leaving on a wonderful driving trip on Sunday. I'm so excited."

Mike carried one of the boxes back to my apartment and I lugged the heavier one. We wished each other well.

Fortunately no one was camped out in front of the office this morning.

When Mike left, I sorted through the two boxes and put most of my office keepsakes on my apartment shelves and tables.

Then I went into the spare room
and pulled out my financial
records.

The check Mike gave me was for
$7,655 which certainly would come
in handy.

There had been one tremendous
advantage in never marrying. My
accumulated savings were quite
hefty. Some of my friends had gone
through costly divorces and were
basically starting over after
being forced to split their assets
and pay outrageous legal bills.

If I felt like it, I certainly
had enough money to retire myself,
although I had no idea how I might
fill my time with no job to go to.

Jokingly, I wondered if $7,655
would be enough to get myself a
penis extension and a case of
Viagra.

I felt that the severance money
should be used to provide myself
with some luxury or other, some
type of fitting reward for
terminating a long career.

Unlike Myrtle, I definitely did
not feel that Lori's tasteless

revenge had inadvertently done me any sort of favor.

Still in a bit of a state of shock, the last thing I wanted to do was mope around my apartment all day.

It was almost one o'clock so I chose to treat myself to a retirement lunch.

I decided to hit my favorite spot, Magnolia's in the Four Queens. I waited patiently by the cashier's counter until a booth became available overlooking the casino. Once again I ordered the meat lover's pizza but this time with a whole pitcher of Old Town Brown dark beer.

If you haven't been to Magnolia's, I have to explain that the front portion of the restaurant sits about seven feet above the casino floor. I had a great view of the blackjack tables and the people walking past me.

While I was throwing back my first glass of beer, and before my food arrived, I noticed a group of three guys on the casino floor who appeared to be gawking up at me.

The next thing I knew they were inside the restaurant standing at my table.

"Hey, man, we recognize you. You're Lance Majestik. Can we get your autograph?"

This was a first. No one in my entire life had ever made such a request.

"Sure, fellows; do you have a pen?"

They whipped out a pen and I duly autographed the various items they placed on my table.

"We caught you on Fat Freddy's show last Friday and you were great," one of the guys gushed.

"I saw Letterman's show last night," a second man interjected," and Dave did his 'Top Ten List' about you. You're a hero, man, for standing up to the abuse that bitch was hurling at you."

"Thanks, guys. It's not all good news, though. I got sacked from my job this morning because of all that publicity. This is my retirement lunch I'm about to drink."

They laughed at my joke and wished me good luck.

Other diners had witnessed the men getting my autograph and several of them timidly approached me and asked who I was. I half lied and said my name was Lance Majestik and that I was a porn star. That stopped them in their tracks and I wasn't asked to do any further signing.

It was almost four o'clock by the time I had polished off the pizza and huge pitcher of beer.

I poured myself home.

Surprisingly I wasn't depressed. So far it appeared that being unemployed wasn't going to drag me down into a deep funk.

CHAPTER NINE (Goodbye Anonymous)

I should probably have turned off the telephone ringer when I got back home, but I was too intoxicated to be sensible.

At six o'clock I turned on the local news.

The lead story was about a casino robbery which took place on the Strip earlier in the day.

The second piece began with a news crew encircling a woman and throwing questions at her. When the lady's face was visible, I almost fell off the couch.

It was Lori and the reporters were hounding her for confirmation that she was the woman responsible for the attacks against me.

The poor girl looked like a deer caught in the headlights of an oncoming truck, and had obviously been blindsided when she arrived at her apartment building after work.

Cornered like a wounded cougar, Lori opted to stand and fight.

"Let me repeat the question, Miss Irwin. Were you responsible for the walking billboard demeaning Lance Majestik and the nude posters plastered all over downtown Las Vegas?"

Like a seasoned politician, Lori lied her panties off and simply replied, "No."

"Then how do you explain these receipts in your name from Budget Bob's Printing Emporium?"

The reporter thrust some papers in Lori's face. She looked at the items for a moment, appeared to be close to panic, but quickly regained her composure and lashed out at me.

"Oh, now I know who you're referring to. I've been trying to put all memories of that loser out of my mind. Yes, of course it was me but I was just doing my civic duty to the women of Las Vegas."

"What do you mean by that?" the reporter queried.

"We girls have to stick together. When one of us encounters a slimy con-man, it's important that we warn our sisters."

"Are you saying that Mr. Majestik somehow tried to swindle you?"

"Exactly! What would you call it when a guy treats you to a nice dinner and then back in his apartment whips out a useless three-inch dick on the pretense that somehow you're going to enjoy playing with it. At the very least I got badly shortchanged. As far as my friends and I are concerned, any guy with such a worthless penis deserves to be exterminated. Lance Majestik is nothing but a disgusting eunuch dressed up in a real man's suit."

"Mr. Majestik actually lost his job today because of the unwanted attention that your little poster campaign caused his employer. What do you have to say about that?"

"That's great news. Maybe now the limp loser will move away and stop disgusting the women of Las Vegas with his tiny excuse for a sexual organ. I know from bitter experience that I'll never get over the horrible shock of seeing 'Little Lance' up close and personal. If the posters have saved even one of my sisters from that frightful fate, then my campaign of truth has been worth it. As a whistleblower, I had a solemn duty to warn other women."

She should have been an actress because Lori then stared straight into the camera and announced, "If you're watching this, Lance, please do women everywhere a favor and feed that horrid, floppy little dick to the nearest garburator."

Having said her piece, Lori then defiantly pushed through the news crew into the lobby of her apartment building.

The news lady was speechless. It was apparent that they were taping live because there was a moment of silent confusion before the station reverted back to the news anchor.

A couple of hours later Lori and her cronies phoned.

"I told you the best was yet to come," a somewhat drunk and sarcastic Lori taunted. "I hope you've already taken my wise advice about the garburator and ground up that hideous midget you laughingly call your pecker."

"Why yes I have, Lori, and I've got some great news for you. I sold Little Lance to the deli so there's still a chance you might wrap your bitchy lips around the little fellow yet. I hope you choke on him."

"Fat chance," she retorted. "He's so tiny; he couldn't even choke a flea."

"You ought to know about such things since your well-used pussy is America's receptacle for crabs, syphilis and all other types of vaginal pestilence."

This time I hung up, determined never to let myself get goaded into another adolescent exchange

with Lori. I resolved to change my
phone number as soon as possible.

CHAPTER TEN (Back to Obscurity)

Finally the next day, being Thursday, some personal good luck drifted my way. It was November 14th and another buffoon had blasted his way into the comedy routines and salacious newscasts of Las Vegas and elsewhere. This time is was a public figure.

The Mayor of Toronto, Rob Ford, was suddenly the preferred butt of jokes, and his outrageous antics pushed Little Lance, Lori and me right off the radar.

Our brief claim to fame was thankfully relegated to the history books.

I obtained a new and unlisted telephone number on Friday morning and haven't heard from Lori since.

I began wearing the wig and beard disguise whenever I ventured out in public. My autograph signing days were over.

With more than ample time on my hands, I wrote a short story about my life with Little Lance, and today I'm publishing it on Amazon.

As a totally unknown author, I'm confident that no one will actually pay good money to read my story. After all, at least 90,000 new Kindle books get published each and every month.

But at least my humiliating experiences have now been recorded for posterity even if the saga gets buried under the giant haystack of published but undiscovered books written by my fellow nobodies.

ABOUT THE AUTHOR

Donald W. Desaulniers is a retired Canadian lawyer who resides in the picturesque small city of Belleville, Ontario with his lovely British wife, Jane. Always a proponent of quantity over quality, Desaulniers has written more than seventy-five novels, most of which relate to the legal profession that everyone loves to loathe. LOVE MOCKS A LIMP DICK was the author's first attempt at bawdy schoolboy humor.

Each of the novels listed below is available as an E-Book and in Paperback form through Amazon.

OTHER WORKS BY THIS AUTHOR

SCHOOLBOY/BAWDY HUMOR

CRAZY OLD LAWYER (A TALKING SKIN TAG)
LOVE MOCKS A LIMP DICK

LEGAL SERIES

SLIMY LAWYER (#1 in Series)
SLIMY SUES AMERICA (#2 in Series)

SLIMY GETS SHAFTED (#3 in Series)
SLIMY GETS DISBARRED (#4 in Series)
SLIMY TASTES THE GOOD LIFE (#5 in Series)
SLIMY LAWYER CHECKS OUT (#6 in Series)

THE WRONG LAWYER (#1 in Series)
SNARKY LAWYERS (#2 in Series)

VANISHING LAWYER (A WORLD WITHOUT ME)
VANISHING LAWYER #2 (UNWANTED WITNESS)
VANISHING LAWYER #3 (FUGITIVE ALIEN)
VANISHING LAWYER #4 (SAVING THE PRESIDENT)
VANISHING LAWYER #5 (SWINDLING SENIORS)
VANISHING LAWYER #6 (SAVING TRUMP AGAIN)

WEIRD LAWYER #1 (NOVICE ATTORNEY)
WEIRD LAWYER #2 (TOUGH TIMES)
WEIRD LAWYER #3 (A PINCH OF JEALOUSY)

LAWYER MURDER MYSTERIES

DIE NOW OLD MAN
SHUT THAT LAWYER UP
PARADE OF DEAD LAWYERS
LUCKY LAWYER
THE TWIN SHADOWS
TERRORIST LAWYER

OTHER LEGAL NOVELS

RICH LAWYER, POOR PRIEST
LOATHING THE LAWYER, LOVING THE LAWYER
LADY LUCK LOVES LAWYERS
THE LORD SNATCHES AWAY
THE CHRISTMAS LAWYER
LAWYER IN THE TOILET
THE LAWYER'S MUSLIM NEIGHBORS
REVENGE DELAYED
DIVERGENT LAWYER

YOUNG BUT NOT STUPID
MYSTERY OF THE OLD DESK
BUYING REDEMPTION
THE CHEAPSKATE TWINS
FAKE LAWYER
NAÏVE LAWYER
THE LIPPY LAWYER'S ROMANCE
TEMPTING THE GOOD LAWYER
BROKE, DISGRACED AND ALONE
A RETIRED LAWYER'S DOOMED ROMANCE
FIFTY YEARS LATER (Hitchhiking in Donald
Trump's America)

ROMANCE NOVELS

BEVY OF BEAUTIES (Finding Love After Loss)
SWEET ROMANCE BACK HOME
LOVE SAVES A LONER

YOUNG ADULT NOVELS

YOUNG BUT NOT STUPID
MYSTERY OF THE OLD DESK
CELESTIAL COINCIDENCE

ACTION NOVELS

CROSSING A RICH MAN (Turning the Tables)
VILE FAMILIES
THE LEFT TACKLE'S CHRISTMAS
ESCAPE FROM EVERYTHING
THE TWIN SHADOWS
ALIEN SPECTATORS
MARTY MARCOTTE'S REVOLVING LIFE

THE TY WARD ADVENTURE SERIES

TY WARD HITS AMERICA (#1 in Series)
TY WARD'S HOLIDAY FROM HELL (#2 in Series)

TY WARD'S NEXT WAR (#3 in Series)
DEADLY WITNESS (#4 in Series)
A YOUNG HOOKER'S THANKS (#5 in Series)
TY WARD'S LAST WAR (#6 in Series)
TY WARD'S SHATTERED PEACE (#7 in Series)
TY WARD'S ROUGH JUSTICE (#8 in Series)

SHORT NOVELS WRITTEN UNDER PEN NAME "DURWARD GARBAGE"

WRONG PLACE, WORST TIME
ABANDONED ALIEN (Space Aliens for Donald Trump)
GOLDEN CHAOS (Stock Market Meltdown)
NASTY MAN (Mr. Jerk)
ALMOST A LAWYER
SQUANDERING MY FORTUNE
REVENGE FROM HER GRAVE
LAWYER ON THE RUN (Panhandling Attorney)
SCORNFUL FAMILY (Eating Insults)